ISBN: 978-0-578-88229-1

Dedication

To my loving husband and best friend, Collin, whom I love more than words can express. To my children who have stretched and taught me so much about life, you are my reason why. Dear family and friends, which are too many to name, I love you. *"We are the sum total of our experiences - be they positive or negative make us the person we are" B.J. Neblett* All of you have so much to do with who I am today, thank you, love you all.

Most importantly, thank you, My Heavenly Father, for your favor.

NOTES FROM THE AUTHOR

Dear Woman of Wisdom,

You are destined for greatness! It's God's design, for He has planted seeds of greatness in each of you. His plan for your life is for those seeds to sprout, grow and produce a life of health and happiness. He has never changed His mind, although you have changed our minds again and again.

The Bible will guide you into your destiny. The LORD has brought many of you from prisons to pulpits, from barstools to church pews, from hopelessness to hope. God's word will separate you from the sting of death, the woes of this world, and it will place you in the flow of His life. Jesus said,

"The words that I speak unto you, they are spirit, and they are life" John 6:63

I genuinely love each of you and want nothing but God's best for your life.

MiMi.

PART ONE:

30 DAYS OF NEW BEGINNINGS

Inspiration for Today

Beautiful Woman of Wisdom,

It is a New Beginning! A New Day! New Hope! Everything is brand new!

Juansen Dizon phrases it like this. *"I hope you realize that every day is a fresh start for you. That every sunrise is a new chapter in your life waiting to be written."*

The Lord phrases it like this. *"You crown the year with your bounty, and your carts overflow with abundance."* Psalm 65:11

Now is the time to start fresh to explore new ideas, work towards your dreams, and make necessary changes. Now is the time to move through the year, day by day, and moment by moment with determination and zeal. Now is the time to leave the shadows of the past in the past! Now is the time!

Enjoy the first day of the rest of your life; love and hugs, MiMi.

Song of the day - I hope you dance – by Lee Ann Womack

Thoughts

Inspiration for Today

Beautiful Woman of Wisdom,

Bless the Lord O, my soul! Here you are, another new day, a new beginning, a fresh-start either phrase you choose means a change.

What change are you considering? What difference would you like to see in your life? Is it a physical, mental, or spiritual change, or are you hoping someone else will change? Does the mere mention of the word change make you nervous or fearful?

I know that change can be frightening because you don't have control. Even the change that you do have control over can bring fear. Embrace change with information, prayer, faith, and courage.

James 1:17 *"Every good gift and every perfect gift is from above, coming down from the Father of lights with whom there is no variation or shadow due to change."*

Enjoy the first day of the rest of your life; love and hugs, MiMi.

Song of the day - A change has come over me – by Hillsong Worship

Thoughts

Inspiration for Today

Beautiful Woman of Wisdom

You're at the beginning of your change; while in the process, be careful of your triggers. What are your triggers? What causes you to come out of character? What drives you to lose your religion?

I'm asking because you need to know your triggers. Controlling your triggers will lead to less stress, less apologizing, better understanding, and communication.

Everyone has those things that cause the hair on the back of the neck to stand up; you're human. Gain an in-depth understanding of yourself; this will lead to a more peaceful life. 1 Corinthians 10:13 *"No temptation has overtaken you that is not common to man. God is faithful, and he will not let you be tempted beyond your ability, but with the temptation, he will also provide the way of escape, that you may be able to endure it."*

Enjoy the first day of the rest of your life, love and hugs, MiMi.

Song of the day - In Control - by Hillsong Worship

Thoughts

Inspiration for Today

Beautiful Woman of Wisdom,

The beauty of a new day! Woman of Wisdom, you can choose to give this day your best effort despite your current situation and because God loves us.

Focus your thoughts on positivity because your thoughts become your words; your words need to be positive, for they speak life and death.

Proverbs 18:21 *"The tongue has the power of life and death."*

The stakes are high. Your words can speak life or death. Your tongues can build you up, or you can tear yourselves down. I am not talking about what you say to others; I speak about what you tell yourselves. Whenever I find my mind entertaining self-defeating thoughts, I stop myself and replace those thoughts with positive ones.

The battle is in your mind. The question is, what's in your mind? What are you feeding your spirit? As you move through your journey in life, you must be mindful of what you see and what you hear, what you read, and indeed the company you keep.

Enjoy the first day of the rest of your life, love and hugs, MiMi.

Song of the day - Never Let Go - by Positive.

Thoughts

Inspiration for Today

Beautiful Woman of Wisdom,

Amazing grace! You are moving through another minute, day, and year, and you are ever-changing, and as you change, the world is changing around you.

Sometimes change goes unnoticed because it's subtle. Change can also be sudden and shocking. Be aware that everything changes and everything will change; it's called life.

You know nothing stays the same except some of your behaviors and your way of thinking; if that is the case, then you're stuck. Growth won't happen when you're stuck? Change is living, and as you live, you should progress; let's embrace change with grace and faithfulness and trust.

Proverb 1:4 *"Let the wise listen and add to their learning, and let the discerning get guidance."*

Enjoy the first day of the rest of your life; love and hugs, MiMi.

Song of the day - Change Me - by Tamela Mann.

Thoughts

Inspiration for Today

Beautiful Woman of Wisdom.

It's time for a new beginning! What does your new beginning look like? When does a new beginning start? Well, it begins now. Why wait?

Why put on hold what you can do today? Why wait until tomorrow? You know that tomorrow is not promised; your new beginning starts now.

You're worthy of a new beginning, a fresh start, guard your minds and don't allow your worth to diminished because of your thoughts or the thoughts of others.

Ephesians 2:10 *"You are God's masterpiece."*

Webster's dictionary defines a "masterpiece" as "a person's greatest work of art" or a "consummate example of skill or excellence."

Enjoy the first day of the rest of your life; love and hugs, MiMi.

Song of the day – Masterpiece - by Deitrick Haddon

Thoughts

Inspiration for Today

Beautiful Woman of Wisdom.

New beginnings start with the renewal of your minds. Let's talk about the renewal; reading the word and spending time with the Lord aids in renewing your mind. What happens when consumed with worry, doubt, confusion, depression, anger, and feelings of condemnation? Those thoughts can cause depression, sadness, and living an unhealthy life.

Those thoughts certainly don't feel like renewal; those thoughts are attacks on the mind. You have to think about what you are thinking about and practice replacing negative thoughts with thoughts of good times, good memories, dreams, visions, and God's promises.

Philippians 4:8 *"Finally, brethren, whatsoever things are true, whatsoever things are honorable, whatsoever things are just, whatsoever things are pure, whatsoever things are lovely, whatsoever things are of good report; if there be any virtue, and if there be any praise, think on these things."*

Enjoy the first day of the rest of your life, love and hugs, MiMi.

Song of the day – No Fear - by Veronica Petrucci

Thoughts

Inspiration for Today

Beautiful Woman of Wisdom,

Remember, we are talking about new beginnings, not waiting to start tomorrow but starting now, working towards your goals, dreams, and visions.

Today is the day!

New Beginnings, don't you love having another day to start fresh? The renewing of your mind, how do you renew the mind? By spending time in the word, spending time with God, and learning from yesterday while living in the present with the expectation of a bright future.

Joshua 1:8 *'Do not let this Book of the Law depart from your mouth;*

Meditate on it day and night so that you may be prosperous and successful."

Enjoy the first day of the rest of your life, love and hugs, MiMi.

Song of the day - This is the day - by Fred Hammond

Thoughts

Inspiration for Today

Beautiful Woman of Wisdom,

It's a Brand New day, again!

Does it feel brand new? Well, it's still a new day no matter how you feel or what you're thinking, so why not embrace it. It may feel hopeless today, but because you have hope and a loving God, you can get up, take up and walk.

John 5:8 *"Then Jesus said to him, "Get up! Pick up your mat and walk."*

Isaiah 41:10 *"fear not, for I am with you; be not dismayed, for I am your God; I will strengthen you, I will help you, I will uphold you with my righteous right hand."*

Enjoy the first day of the rest of your life, love and hugs, MiMi.

Song of the day - Another New Day - by Georgia Mass Choir

Thoughts

Inspiration for Today

Beautiful Woman of Wisdom,

New Day! New Beginning! Renewed Mind! This new day is precious, with its hopes and dreams; let's not waste a moment on yesterdays' mistakes or yesterdays' lack; let's begin today fresh!

Each new day begins with no rules and no limitations except for the rules and limits you set. Today is filled with endless possibilities!

New Day! New Beginning! Renewed Mind!

Psalm 51:10-12 *"God, make a fresh start in me, shape a Genesis week from the chaos of my life. Don't throw me out with the trash or fail to breathe holiness in me. Bring me back from gray exile, put a fresh wind in my sails!"*

Enjoy the first day of the rest of your life, love and hugs, MiMi.

Song of the day - Hallelujah - by Alexandra Burke.

Thoughts

Inspiration for Today

Beautiful Woman of Wisdom,

It's a New Day! New Beginnings! A Renewed Mind! If you are reading this, then guess what. It's the first day of the rest of your life; I hope you're excited.

If you didn't start yesterday, then begin today; your years will never take away your chance for a new beginning. It's only the beginning right now. So dreams can still come true, vision can always come to fruition. We've talked about renewing our minds in conjunction with a new beginning because that is where it starts.

Lisa Nichols stated, *"Your thoughts and your feelings create your life. It will always be that way. Guaranteed!"*

Isaiah 43:18-19 *"Remember not the former things, nor consider the things of old. Behold, I am doing a new thing; now it springs forth, do you not perceive it? I will make a way in the wilderness and rivers in the desert."*

Enjoy the first day of the rest of your life, love and hugs, MiMi.

Song of the day - Renewal Song - by Bonnie Kane

Thoughts

Inspiration for Today

Beautiful Woman of Wisdom,

Be encouraged, and remember that you can start fresh, begin again, move on, etc., whenever you choose, any second, minute, hour, or day.

It's great to begin a New Year with goals and aspirations; it's that time of year when most people are full of optimism, and many people make grand promises to themselves; make goals about what they're going to do in the New Year.

However, statics show that approximately 50% of Americans make New Year resolutions, and around 10% complete them. So even if you made resolutions and you failed, so what every day is a New Beginning. So, begin again, just start.

Philippians 3:13-14 *"Brothers and sisters, I do not consider myself yet to have taken hold of it. But one thing I do: Forgetting what is behind and straining toward what is ahead, I press on toward the goal to win the prize for which God has called me heavenward in Christ Jesus."*

Enjoy the first day of the rest of your life, love and hugs, MiMi.

Song of the day - New Season - by Israel & New Bread

Thoughts

Inspiration for Today

Beautiful Woman of Wisdom,

This is the day the Lord has made. Let us rejoice and be glad in it. We are talking about new beginnings; astonishingly, we are privileged to have a fresh start every day that we open our eyes.

No matter what yesterday brought, you slept, you rose, yesterday is history, and it will never come again.

Today you get to start afresh, renewed, and if you chose yesterday, sadness, madness, or despair, then you're choosing the past.

When I read this quote, *"Never put off till tomorrow what you can do today."* Lord Chesterfield. I knew I had to share this with my sisters because every day is a new day, and it can be beautiful.

Beautiful Woman of Wisdom, this is the first day of the rest of your beautiful life; enjoy it because you are worthy.

Ecclesiastes 3:11 *"He has made everything beautiful in its time. He has also set eternity in the hearts of men, yet they cannot fathom what God has done from beginning to end."*

Enjoy the first day of the rest of your life, love and hugs, MiMi.

Song of the day - God Will Make a Way - by Deon Moen

Thoughts

Inspiration for Today

Beautiful Woman of Wisdom,

God gifted you with new mercies every day. I know there are times when it doesn't feel like new mercy; the good news is that it is a new day, and it's filled with the promises of God. The Lord will never leave you nor forsake you, although there are times in your life that you feel alone.

He will always be with you even to the end of the age. When this day is over, He will be with you, and when this life is over, He will be with you. No matter how hard it gets, the sun will shine again, and with each new day, there are new mercies. You can survive whatever life has for you because your God is with you. His promises are true.

Laminations 3:22-23 *"The steadfast love of the Lord never ceases; his mercies never come to an end; they are new every morning; great is your faithfulness."*

Enjoy the first day of the rest of your life, love and hugs, MiMi.

Song of the day - New Every Morning - by Audrey Assad

Thoughts

Inspiration for Today

Beautiful Woman of Wisdom,

A new beginning is not always welcome; there are times when a new beginning happens: death meaning life without a loved one, divorce meaning life without a loved one, loss of a job, children growing up, and leaving home.

You may long for things to remain the same, for nothing to change the problem with that desire is that change is a constant, and it is coming, so embrace it. So what do you do when a New Beginning happens?

Joshua 1:19 *"Have I not commanded you? Be strong and courageous. Do not be frightened, and do not be dismayed, for the Lord your God is with you wherever you go."*

There it is; you are to be strong and courageous, for your God is with you.

Enjoy the first day of the rest of your life, love and hugs, MiMi.

Song of the day - Everything Must Change - by George Benson

Thoughts

Inspiration for Today

Beautiful Woman of Wisdom,

New Beginning, New Start, New Day, whatever you call this day, let's start with thankfulness. Beginning the day with Gratitude will set the tone for your day. Let's declare the direction of your day instead of wandering into it.

Starting your day with Gratitude immediately places a smile on your face, peace in your spirit, and faith in your walk.

Psalm 100 *"Make a joyful noise unto the Lord, all ye lands. Serve the Lord with gladness: come before his presence with singing. Know ye that the Lord he is God: it is he that hath made us, and not you yourselves; you are his people and the sheep of his pasture. Enter into his gates with thanksgiving, and into his courts with praise: be thankful unto him, and bless his name. For the Lord is good; his mercy is everlasting, and his truth endureth to all generations."*

Enjoy the first day of the rest of your life, love and hugs, MiMi.

Song of the day - Psalm 100 - by Chris Tomlin

Thoughts

Inspiration for Today

Beautiful Woman of Wisdom,

Forward and backward back and forth around and around, does this cycle sound familiar? Many of you have lived your life and are living your lives in this cycle. This behavior is inconsistent with a new beginning and a new direction.

You can build on your past mistakes and use them to propel forward. Close the door to your past; something's you will never forget; mistakes, choices, and some ugly actions, but you don't have to live there or dwell there.

Don't allow your past to steal your energy, time, or your joy and future.

1 Corinthians 2:9 *"However, as it is written: "What no eye has seen, what no ear has heard, and what no human mind has conceived" -- the things God has prepared for those who love him."*

Enjoy the first day of the rest of your life, love and hugs, MiMi.

Song of the day - Let it go - by DeWayne Woods

Thoughts

Inspiration for Today

Beautiful Woman of Wisdom,

It's a New Day; how wonderful it is to wake up and know that you can decide to move forward! It's here the first day of the rest of your life.

The Bible states in Luke 1:78, *"A new day will dawn on us from above because your God is loving and merciful."*

Let's live each moment of this day deliberately with Gratitude and Thankfulness. In a world of uncertainties, it's good to know you have a heavenly Father who proves his love by keeping His Word and His Promises. There is no circumstance, tragedy, or trial that He hasn't anticipated and promises to see us through. So live Woman of Wisdom!

Psalm 73:26 *"My flesh and my heart may fail, but God is the strength of my heart and my portion forever."*

Enjoy the first day of the rest of your life, love and hugs, MiMi.

Song of the day - How Great is Your God - by Chris Tomlin.

Thoughts

Inspiration for Today

Beautiful Woman of Wisdom,

Time to Rise and Shine! Are you familiar with the song? I'm talking about the traditional version, Rise and Shine give God the glory, rise and shine give God the praise, how do you shine?

Do you shine brightly enough to encourage another person? Are you full of energy and positivity? If not, why not? It's a new day filled with possibilities - filled with opportunities, filled with hope. Rise and Shine!

Matthew 5:16 *"Let your light so shine before men, that they may see your good works, and glorify your Father which is in heaven."*

1 Thessalonians 5:11 *"Therefore encourage one another and build each other up, just as you are doing."*

Enjoy the first day of the rest of your life, love and hugs, MiMi.

Song of the day - Rise and Shine Give God the Glory - by Dionne Warwick

Thoughts

Inspiration for Today

Beautiful Woman of Wisdom.

The Lord made this day; let's rejoice and be thankful! New Beginnings! What limitations have you put on this New Day?

So often, you hinder yourselves by placing limits on your day before it even starts. You can't begin a day with limitations from yesterday. Too many of you are trying to live this New Beginning the same way you lived yesterday. You have to reach up to the next level with confidence and determination. You have to speak those things that are not as if they were.

Romans 4:17. *"You start out in a world created by others, but gradually over time, you change that world into one of your creation."*

Psalm 118:24 *"This is the day the Lord has made; you will rejoice and be glad in it."*

Enjoy the first day of the rest of your life, love and hugs, MiMi.

Song of the day - This Is the Day - by Fred Hammond

Thoughts

Inspiration for Today

Beautiful Woman of Wisdom.

New Beginnings, my prayer, and hope for you are that you embrace this day. It's so exciting to awake to a fresh start, a clean slate, another chance.

You need faith, not fear, to enjoy the journey while moving towards your destination. Yes, you have a new day, and it comes with instructions, and these instructions teach us how to embrace this present.

1 Peter 3:10-12 states, *"Whoever wants to embrace life and see the day fill up with good, here's what you do: Say nothing evil or hurtful; Snub evil and cultivate good; run after peace for all you're worth. God looks on all this with approval, listening and responding well to what he's asked; But he turns his back on those who do evil things".*

Enjoy the first day of the rest of your life, love and hugs, MiMi.

Song of the day - New Day - by Kenny Eldrige

Thoughts

Inspiration for Today

Beautiful Woman of Wisdom,

Have you ever struggled to keep moving forward? Have you heard other women speak of the struggle to keep moving forward, move past it, get over it, and push through it?

It's quite simply one foot in front of the other, and eventually, you'll look back and be amazed at how far you've come. Depend on the Lord to carry you through.

There is a song by David Guetta & Sia Lyrics, "One foot in front of the other, one breath leads to another, yeah just keep moving. Look within for the strength today. Listen now for the voice to say, just keep moving."

Genesis 5:24. *"Enoch walked with God; then, he was no more because God took him away."*

What a blessed way to go. The bible talks of walking humbly, walking in the light, walking with the wise, walking in counsel, walking together, and walking on water. WALK IT OUT!

Enjoy the first day of the rest of your life, love and hugs, MiMi.

Song of the day - Walk It out – by P-Phraze

Thoughts

Inspiration for Today

Beautiful Woman of Wisdom,

It's a new day! Whoop, Whoop, Whoop, you have the opportunity to start again and get it right or keep doing it right. Do you know that the days of the week have meanings? Historically for Christians, each day of the week has its spiritual theme. What does each day mean to you?

How are you spending your seven new days? Are they spent daydreaming, wishing, or procrastinating? If you think about today and the choices you make, it will make a difference in your tomorrow.

Jeremiah 29:11, *"For I know the plans I have for you," declares the LORD, "plans to prosper you and not to harm you, plans to give you hope and a future."*

Enjoy the first day of the rest of your life, love and hugs, MiMi.

Song of the day - Living Hope - by Phil Wickham

Thoughts

Inspiration for Today

Beautiful Woman of Wisdom,

New beginnings can begin at any time; a fresh start can begin all day long. How many times have you regretted your actions? You did something that could have been detrimental to your health, finances, or relationships? Can I tell you that you have a Father that sits high and looks low and has the capability of repairing the damage?

More than that, He is capable of renewing your mind, body, and especially your spirit. He is the mender of the brokenhearted, and He is the lifter of your head.

Whenever you feel low and think there is no tomorrow, remember your Father will be there in that low place to comfort and lift you. As long as He is with you, you can do all things, even begin again. All you need to do is seek Him. Did you know that he looked for you first?

Psalm 139:8 *"If I Make My Bed in Hell: "If I ascend up into heaven, thou art there: if I make my bed in hell, behold, thou art there."*

John 15:16 *"You did not choose me, but I chose you and appointed you to go and bear fruit fruit that will last."*

Enjoy the first day of the rest of your life, love and hugs, MiMi.

Song of the day - You Keep Hope Alive - by Mandisa Jon Reddick

Thoughts

Inspiration for Today

Beautiful Woman of Wisdom,

Today is the first day of the rest of your life! The Lord has given us a new day. He has given a Second Chance to Make Another Impression, an opportunity to get it together, and for that, you should CELEBRATE!

How do you move on? How do you start this new day? You begin this day remembering what is important and necessary: Love, Faith & Hope. Hope in the promises of God. Faith that He will do what He promises and Love for your Lord and Savior and your fellow man. Remember, you serve God by serving humanity.

1 Corinthians 13:4-5 *"Love is patient and kind; love does not envy or boast; it is not arrogant or rude. It does not insist on its own way; it is not irritable or resentful; it does not rejoice at wrongdoing."*

Hebrews 11:1 *"Now faith is the substance of things hoped for, the evidence of things not seen."*

Enjoy the first day of the rest of your life, love and hugs, MiMi.

Song of the day - God of a Second Chance - by Hezekiah Walker

Thoughts

Inspiration for Today

Beautiful Woman of Wisdom,

Let's talk about "The Push" if you're pushing, you should know where you want to go? Let's not just PUSH through the day but let's PUSH with a destination in mind, a focused direction, and a determination.

Life can be hard sometimes. PUSH! You all come across tough times. PUSH! I don't feel like it. PUSH! Life isn't fair. PUSH! Remember, beautiful woman of wisdom; you are not PUSHING alone.

Proverbs 16:9 *"The human mind plans the way, but the Lord directs the steps."*

Isaiah 40:30-31 *"Even youths grow tired and weary, and young men stumble and fall, but those who hope in the LORD will renew their strength. They will soar on wings like eagles; they will run and not grow weary, they will walk and not be faint."*

Enjoy the first day of the rest of your life, love and hugs, MiMi.

Song of the day - Pull/Push - by Hillsong

Thoughts

Inspiration for Today

Beautiful Woman of Wisdom,

As you awake to a new day, exercise faith over fear. I decided to exercise my faith in step on my fear! The Lord is faithful, and He can do exceeding and abundantly far more than our minds can even comprehend. You're in a mess, you're amid unemployment, and you're grieving; life seems uncertain, He is able.

I understand that it may seem simple to write these words, but I truly understand what it feels like to walk in uncertainty, and I also have experienced the beauty of our Lord's grace and mercy.

1 John 4:18 *"There is no fear in love, but perfect love casts out fear. For fear has to do with punishment, and whoever fears has not been perfected in love."*

Enjoy the first day of the rest of your life, love and hugs, MiMi.

Song of the day - You've come this far by faith – by Donnie McClurkin

Thoughts

Inspiration for Today

Beautiful Woman of Wisdom,

I call you beautiful because you are lovely! You may not feel beautiful today, your eyes may be puffy, or perhaps you don't have much get up and go, and that's ok. The Lord said in Psalm 105:4, ***"Look to the Lord and his strength; seek his face always."***

Who or what are you seeking today? The Lord has all the answers to your questions. Look no further, for He loves you with an everlasting love.

Psalm 29:11 ***"May the Lord Give strength to his people! May the Lord bless his people with peace!"***

The Lord loves you, and He does what He says He will do. Teach us, Lord, to be more willing to abide in you as you abide in us, for you are faithful.

Enjoy the first day of the rest of your life, love and hugs, MiMi.

Song of the day – You're Beautiful - by Phil Wickham

Thoughts

START HERE

Inspiration for Today

Beautiful Woman of Wisdom,

Motivation! How do you stay motivated day after day, issue after issue, lack of or plenty? How?

The Bible speaks of being content in Philippians; many of you struggle with this. To be content in any and every situation is to be at peace in every condition. Most things are out of your control (although you think you're in control), learning to be content and keeping your faith in every situation is key to having peace of mind.

Philippians 4:11-12 *"I am not saying this because I am in need, for I have learned to be content whatever the circumstances. I know what it is to be in need, and I know what it is to have plenty. I have learned the secret of being content in any and every situation, whether well fed or hungry, whether living in plenty or in want."*

Enjoy the first day of the rest of your life, love and hugs, MiMi.

Song of the day - I Understand - by Smokie Norful.

Thoughts

Inspiration for Today

Beautiful Woman of Wisdom,

Everyday wisdom! Have you wondered why I often say make this day count? It's easy to fall by the wayside, depending on what you're facing. Falling by the wayside means you fail to persist in an endeavor or undertaking, goals, or commitments.

The Bible speaks about the Israelites desire to return to Egypt; when the journey became difficult, the 40-day journey turned into years. There will be times that you begin "heading towards Egypt."

In other words, you start gravitating toward old behaviors or the things of the world instead of staying focused and anchored to God. Don't allow doubt, fear or your actions to disrupt your journey. You can make it count daily. Now let's live.

Proverb 3:5 *"Trust in the Lord with all of your heart, and lean not on your own understanding"*

Enjoy the first day of the rest of your life, love and hugs, MiMi.

Song of the day - I Will Rise - The Wisdom of God – by Chris Tomlin

Thoughts

PART TWO:

30 DAYS 0F ENJOY YOUR LIFE

Inspiration for Today

Beautiful Woman of Wisdom,

It's your life, so live it! Well, it is the end of our first 30 days, and yes, it's the beginning of a new day. I hope yesterday was good where your dreams came true, your prayers answered, and your vision manifested. If not, it's ok you are still in the race; the Lord promises to walk with you, so that settles it!

It doesn't matter what you didn't complete yesterday; all that matters is right now. Begin to move in the direction of your dream, your vision, and your purpose. Do not doubt; only believe for now is the appointed time.

John 10:10 *"The thief comes only to steal and kill and destroy. I came that they may have life and have it abundantly."*

Habakkuk 2:*3 "For the revelation awaits an appointed time; it speaks of the end and will not prove false. Though it lingers, wait for it; it will certainly come and will not delay."*

It's your life, so live! Love and hugs, MiMi.

Song of the day - Abundant Life – by Deitrick Haddon

Thoughts

Inspiration for Today

Beautiful Woman of Wisdom,

How are you feeling about your life today? Is it everything you hoped it be? Remember making decisions outside of God's will affects the quality of your life. You struggled to move forward in life because things didn't work out in your marriage, jobs, family, and now what? It's still your life; how do you want to live?

Each day you wake up, you should be excited; you should be looking forward with gratefulness because you have the opportunity to work on your goals, vision, and plans; these things bring hope to life.

Habakkuk 2:2 *"And the Lord answered me: "Write the vision; make it plain on tablets, so he may run who reads it."*

Psalm 118:24 *"This is the day that the Lord has made; let us rejoice and be glad in it."*

It's your life, so live! Love and hugs, MiMi.

Song of the day - My life is in your hands - by Kirk Franklin.

Thoughts

Inspiration for Today

Beautiful Woman of Wisdom,

The love the Lord has for His daughters is comforting. Say with me:

"I am the daughter of a King that is not moved by the world. For my, God is with me and goes before me. I do not fear because I am His." Adonai Elohim

His ever-present help in the time of need is His promises manifested in your lives. Life experiences may not be as you planned, but the ever-present help you receive from the Lord keeps you, and knowing He loves you is peace to the soul. There is no need to fear; you can walk in faith and love because of Him.

Love Life!

Psalm 34:4 *"I sought the Lord, and he answered me he delivered me from all my fears."*

John 3:16 *"For God so loved the world that he gave his one and only Son, that whoever believes in him shall not perish but have eternal life."*

It's your life, so life! Love and hugs, MiMi.

Song of the day - Faithful God - by Zach Neese

Thoughts

Inspiration for Today

Beautiful Woman of Wisdom,

Knowledge is useless if you don't apply it to your daily walk. It's easy to forget the knowledge you've gained in your walk with the Lord when life throws a curve. Steadfast and unmovable no matter what.

Life can be challenging, and you may find yourselves at a point where you question your faith, your purpose, and ask why. If you look back over your lives, take the time to reflect genuinely, you will gain strength because you can see the grace and love of the Lord throughout the years.

"Those who walk with God, always reach their destination." Henry Ford.

Corinthians 15:58 ***"Therefore, my dear brothers and sisters, stand firm. Let nothing move you. Always give yourselves fully to the work of the Lord because you know that your labor in the Lord is not in vain."***

It's your life, so live! Love and hugs, MiMi.

Song of the day - Be Ye Steadfast - by La Norris McFadden.

Thoughts

Inspiration for Today

Beautiful Woman of Wisdom,

It is your life! It is your decision to live it and make the best of it. How often do you do things because you're told you should or because that's how it's always been done?

Many of your beliefs and actions are what you were taught growing up. You should not behave that way, you should go to church, you should eat your vegetables. There are so many *"you should"* the question is, should you do it? Or do you want to do that? Can you truly live your best life if you live what you should do instead of what you want to do, what you are born to do, and what you are called to do?

Hebrews 12:1-2 *"Therefore, since you are surrounded by such a great cloud of witnesses, let us throw off everything that hinders and the sin that so easily entangles. And let us run with perseverance the race marked out for us, fixing your eyes on Jesus, the pioneer and perfecter of faith. For the joy set before him, he endured the cross, scorning its shame, and sat down at the right hand of the throne of God."*

It's your life, so live it! Love and hugs, MiMi.

Song of the day – You are the Living Word - by Fred Hammond & RFC

Thoughts

Inspiration for Today

Beautiful Woman of Wisdom,

This is the day the Lord has made; rejoice and be glad in it. As you go through the seasons of life, you will find yourselves dealing with trials and tribulations.

Remember that trouble doesn't always last, and if you hold on to God's unchanging hand, you will make it through. He promises that you will not get burnt when you go through the fire, and when you go through the flood, the waters will not overtake you.

Do not let your heart be troubled; embrace patience and keep your faith. Have faith in the one who said, *Let there be light!* And the light came on in a dark place, and a universe was born. Remember He, who began a good work in you, is faithful to complete it.

James 1:2-5 ***"My brethren, count it all joy when you fall into various trials, knowing that the testing of your faith produces patience. But let patience have its perfect work, that you may be perfect and complete, lacking nothing."***

It's your life, so live it! Love and hugs, MiMi.

Song of the day - This Is the Day - by Fred Hammond

Thoughts

Inspiration for Today

Beautiful Woman of Wisdom,

Life can bring challenging times; that seems to last forever; when you look back, you realize they didn't. Life is ebb and flow.

It is the Lord who brought you through, and because of His grace, you're still standing. God made the earth out of chaos; how much more will He do for His children.

Genesis 1:2 *"The earth was without form and void, and darkness was over the face of the deep." So, if your life is chaotic, currently remember who you are and walk in faith."*

Proverbs 3:19-20 *"The Lord by wisdom founded the earth; by understanding, he established the heavens; by knowledge, the deeps broke forth, and the clouds drop down the dew."*

It's your life, so live it! Love and hugs, MiMi.

Song of the day - Don't Look Back - by Josh Wilson.

Thoughts

Inspiration for Today

Beautiful Woman of Wisdom,

It's your life, so live it by making a difference. Martin Luther King, Jr.'s holiday is when you celebrate the life and legacy of a man who brought hope, a man who made a difference; it was his life, and he lived it.

You can make a difference! You can affect those around you and the situations you encounter. You can bring hope amid confusion; it's your response that will make a difference amid chaos. You can respond in kind (in the same way) to adverse situations or bring wisdom to the problem. Unfortunately, living in today's world, you hear and see more negative things than positive ones, but you can make a difference by remembering who you are.

"Never underestimate the difference YOU can make in the lives of others. Step forward, reach out, and help." Pablo.

Ephesians 3:20 ***"Now to him who is able to do immeasurably more than all you ask or imagine, according to his power that is at work within us."***

It's your life, so live it! Love and hugs, MiMi.

Song of the day - You Can Make a Difference - by Jaci Velasquez.

Thought

Inspiration for Today

Beautiful Woman of Wisdom,

I think you can agree that life is filled with stories that are filled with words, right? Throughout your life, you have experienced the pain of words, and you have given pain with the words you have used. Words are like toothpaste once there out - there is no putting them back. You are called to bring life and hope to people with your speech, not to bring harm.

Proverbs 12:18 *"The words of the reckless pierce like swords, but the tongue of the wise brings healing." Reckless words pierce like a sword."*

Those are the messy toothpaste words. They hurt people. They can make a mess in your lives and the lives of others, *"but the tongue of the wise brings healing."* Let's do some healing.

Proverbs 21:23 *"Watch your words and hold your tongue; you'll save yourself a lot of grief."*

It's your life, so live it! Love and hugs, MiMi.

Song of the day - Still I Rise - by Yolanda Adams,

Thoughts

Inspiration for Today

Beautiful Woman of Wisdom,

What matters most to you? How long you live, or how you lived? What matters most, using your voice to be heard or your voice being heard? Some people use their voices to be heard (all of us think we have something to say); it doesn't matter what the topic; they want their voice heard.

Some people have a voice that has substance, relevance, and purpose. Which one are you? How are you living your life? What are you speaking into the ears of those you encounter? Speak with a purpose, not on purpose. The Word of God speaks about the foolishness of just talking.

Ephesians 5:4 *"Let there be no filthiness nor foolish talk nor crude joking, which are out of place, but instead let there be thanksgiving."*

Proverbs 15:2 *"The tongue of the wise adorns knowledge, but the mouth of the fool gushes folly."*

It's your life, so live it! Love and hugs, MiMi. .

Song of the day - You Are Life - by Hillsong Worship

Thoughts

Inspiration for Today

Beautiful Woman of Wisdom,

Is your objective to use wisdom in every aspect of your life? If yes, your question may be, how? Using your life experiences, the Word of God and things you've learned from others will help you walk wisely. Situations of life: breakups, changing friendships, failures, divorce, losing a job, getting older, getting injured, falling sick these things develop wisdom; let's keep growing despite the situations of life.

Many wise women have a history of overcoming adversity; they faced significant challenges in their lives, but instead of feeling defeated and victimized by their circumstances, they positively dealt with them and kept living.

Proverbs 8: 1-3 *"Can't you hear the voice of wisdom? She is standing at the city gates and every fork in the road, and the door of every house. Listen to what she says:"*

It's your life, so live it! Love and hugs, MiMi.

Song of the day - Walking in the Light - by Hillsong Worship.

Thoughts

Inspiration for Today

Beautiful Woman of Wisdom,

The voice of wisdom, let's talk about reasoning with yourself.

Everyone reasons with themselves; some of you talk out loud, and some of you don't; perhaps you do both. Using reasoning and not emotion will lead to better choices in your lives.

You often hear the saying; Live on Purpose. To live on purpose means thinking clearly and rationally when making decisions. The act of reasoning is thinking about something logically and sensibly, which is a key to living on purpose.

Let's not deceive ourselves with false reasoning. The Bible warns about this danger in James 1:22 ***"But be ye doers of the word, and not hearers only, deceiving your own selves."***

Charles Edge "Let's not be deceived by your own reasoning."

It's your life, so live it! Love and hugs, MiMi.

Song of the day – Reason - by Unspoken

Thoughts

Inspiration for Today

Beautiful Woman of Wisdom,

It's your life, so live it with wisdom. You know the Fruits of the Spirit, but do you understand how to apply the knowledge of the fruit? Fruits of the spirit: love, peace, joy, kindness, gentleness, goodness, patience, faithfulness, and self-control. Do you see the anchor? Love is the anchor; the center is Love (God is Love).

People may love you, not because of what you did but because of what you didn't do. Don't become confused by this statement, of course; what you do matters; however, what matters more is what you don't do.

The Bible instructs us to be patient and gentle with others and demonstrate understanding regardless of the issue. Love is patient! The word love is used so often and, at times, with very little thought or emotion. "I love chocolate. I love that sports team. I love playing games. I love my friends. I love the summer. I love my life. The question is, how are you living? Are the fruits your guide?

It's your life, so live it! Love and hugs, MiMi.

Song of the day - Our God Is Love - by Hillsong Worship.

Thoughts

Inspiration for Today

Beautiful Woman of Wisdom,

An inconsistent lifestyle will not bear much fruit.

Inconsistent meaning erratic, changeable, or unpredictable is that living; if so, at what cost? Have you thought about your life, your walk, your ways?

Your walk with the Lord should always be consistent; you can't allow day-to-day pressures or life issues to influence your walk.

Sometimes, you'll experience inconsistent behavior, which is normal, but it can't become your standard. Fight to stay focus!

Romans 13:13 *"Let us walk with decency, as in the daylight: not in carousing and drunkenness; not in sexual impurity and promiscuity; not in quarreling and jealousy."*

Ephesians 2:10 *"For you are His creation, created in Christ Jesus for good works, which God prepared ahead of time so that you should walk in them."*

It's your life, so live it! Love and hugs, MiMi.

Song of the day - Withholding - by William McDowell.

Thoughts

Inspiration for Today

Beautiful Woman of Wisdom,

The "it's" of life is anything you are going through that may cause you to worry. We all experience the "it's" in life. Life is ever-changing, and at times, you can't find the rhythm, reason, or understanding, and you're left wondering.

There will be times that your actions put you in the middle of the "it's." Regardless of how you arrived, what's important is how you handle it. It's not easy when you're in *"it,"* but it's possible to keep the faith.

Are you experiencing "it"? Please remember that your Heavenly Father is in control. Exercise your faith by working through "it." don't turn your head from "it" faith is like a muscle and needs to be exercised. Faith is the gift of God. It is not of yourself; you receive it from him.

Luke 8:25 *"Where is your faith?" he asked his disciples in fear and amazement, they asked one another, "Who is this? He commands even the winds and the water, and they obey him."*

It's your life, so live it! Love and hugs, MiMi.

Song of the day - You've come this far by faith - by Donnie McClurkin.

Thoughts

Inspiration for Today

Beautiful Woman of Wisdom,

"It" referring to a storm that is raging in your lives, a problem or situation that is difficult to handle, painful, and sad. After a storm, the result can lead to growth, peace, and understanding, depending on how you handle the storm.

Why do you run from your storms? You're intelligent, and you know that life has its ups and downs. Instead of fighting, why not glide through the storm knowing that God is with you. All things are possible with God.

"After the rain, the sun will reappear. There is life. After the pain, the joy will still be here." Walt Disney Company

John 6:13 ***"I have told you all this so that you may have peace in me. Here on earth, you will have many trials and sorrows. But take heart because I have overcome the world."***

Ponder on your life and be grateful because you're still standing, and you live to glide another day.

It's your life, so live it! Love and hugs, MiMi.

Song of the day - Peace in the midst of the storm - by Shirley Caesar

Thoughts

Inspiration for Today

Beautiful Woman of Wisdom,

Are you gliding or fighting through your storm? Some storms we need to push harder through and exercise that faith muscle.

Dealing with storms of life can affect your attitude towards others; there is no excuse to have a bad attitude, you have to be stronger than that. Storms happen to us all. It is impartial, inevitable, and can be purposeful. I urge you to exercise the muscle of faith!

James 1:3 *"Faith is not immune to trials; it is fueled by trials."*

James 1:2-4 *"Count it all joy, my brothers, when you meet trials of various kinds, for you know that the testing of your faith produces steadfastness. And let steadfastness have its full effect, that you may be perfect and complete, lacking in nothing."*

It's your life, so live it! Love and hugs, MiMi.

Song of the day - Faith's Song - by Amy Wadge

Thoughts

Inspiration for Today

Beautiful Woman of Wisdom,

It's going to be a lovely day, depending on how you go through the storm. I read these words, rebalance, reawaken, rethink, rekindle, redefine, rediscover, reimagine, relive, repurpose, reinvent, reclaim & recapture. Several of these words speak to me personally, and I'm wondering what about you?

I realize that for me to handle my storm, I need to rethink, redefine, and recapture some things in my life. It's about having a healthy approach to the storms in your lives with the full understanding that God is the author and finisher of your faith and your life.

Hebrews 12:2 *"looking unto Jesus, the author, and finisher of your faith, who for the joy that was set before Him endured the cross, despising the shame and has sat down at the right hand of the throne of God."*

It's your life, so live it! Love and hugs, MiMi.

Song of the day - Here I Am - by Tamela Mann

Thoughts

Inspiration for Today

Beautiful Woman of Wisdom,

The shadows of life. Your shadow will always follow you, and the brighter the sun, the more visible the shadow. What about those shadows of your past that continue to follow you no matter how far forward you travel?

No matter how much you change, either people or yourselves continue to recall your past shadows. It's time to release yourselves from the shadows that hinder you, time to free yourselves from self-made chains; it's time to release!

2 Corinthians 3:17 *"Now the Lord is the Spirit, and where the Spirit of the Lord is, there is freedom."*

John 8:36 *"So if the Son sets you free, you will be free indeed.*

It's your life, so live it! Love and hugs, MiMi.

Song of the day - Shadows Lyric Video - by VOUS Worship

Thoughts

Inspiration for Today

Beautiful Woman of Wisdom,

Are you living a focused and fearless life, Woman of Wisdom? Yes, it's normal to fear; however, it's not expected as believers to live an unfocused and fearful life. Living this way is contrary to the gift of love, faith, and the promises of God.

Being focused means directing a great deal of attention, interest, or activity towards a particular aim. If you focus on your goals, dreams, and visions, there will be little time for fear.

Isaiah 43:1 *"Don't fear, for I have redeemed you; I have called you by name; you are Mine."*

When you understand where you are, where you're going, your fear decreases, and your faith increases; the Bible has powerful scriptures that bring peace to mind and subdues those unpleasant thoughts. All things are possible, even living a life of peace without fear.

It's your life, so live it! Love and hugs, MiMi.

Song of the day – Fearless - by Jasmine Murray

Thoughts

Inspiration for Today

Beautiful Woman of Wisdom,

It's your life, are you living it? Is your life a whirlwind of busyness? Busy at work, busy thinking about life, busy planning, busy with family, busy doing nothing just busy, busy. The busyness of life can be exhausting and will affect and disrupt your life.

It would be best if you remembered that focus and consistency are the keys to an abundant life. Let your busyness be about our Heavenly Father's business, which is serving Him by serving humanity.

Philippians 4:8 *"Finally, brethren, whatsoever things are true, whatsoever things are honest, whatsoever things are just, whatsoever things are pure, whatsoever things are lovely, whatsoever things are of good report; if there be any virtue, and if there be any praise, think on these things."*

It's your life, so live it! Love and hugs, MiMi.

Song of the day – Breathe - by Jonny Diaz

Thoughts

Inspiration for Today

Beautiful Woman of Wisdom,

Your daily life consists of constant communication; phone, email, social media, and instant messaging. To stay on track, you need to learn to listen to understand, not to respond. Listening is arguably one of the most challenging skills in communication, and it's getting harder. A life filled with noise!

Noise can be distracting, intrusive, and irrelevant, and noise can drown out what's important to hear. I read a statement by Andy Eklund that said, *"there is a lag between what you hear and what you understand."*

Depending upon the individual, it could be between a few seconds to up to a minute. If this is factual, how do you listen to understand? It will take a deliberate effort and focused attention to hear what others are saying.

Typically, while others speak, you're forming opinions and responses based on your beliefs, values, and experience. If you value the person you're speaking with, you should respect them enough to focus on their words and not your thoughts.

Mark 4:24 ***"And he said to them, "Pay attention to what you hear: with the measure you use, it will be measured to you, and still more will be added to you."***

It's your life, so live it! Love and hugs, MiMi.

Song of the day – Noise - by Brian Courtney Wilson

Thoughts

Inspiration for Today

Beautiful Woman of Wisdom,

It's your life, so live it. How are you living? Are you living for others or through others? Is your life filled with commitments that rob you of your time?

Believe it or not, there is such a thing as being too giving. I've found that some women tend to over-promise and under-deliver; perhaps it's because they say what they think others want to hear? Maybe they think they can deliver? It would be wise to weigh the situation before committing. It's your life, so live it.

Luke 14:28-30 *"For which of you, desiring to build a tower, does not first sit down and count the cost, whether he has enough to complete it? Otherwise, when he has laid a foundation and is not able to finish, all who see it begin to mock him, saying, 'This man began to build and was not able to finish."*

It's your life, so live it! Love and hugs, MiMi.

Song of the day - Livin' - by The Clark Sisters

Thoughts

Inspiration for Today

Beautiful Woman of Wisdom,

Whatever the season of life you're in, strive to be content while you wait for the harvest, meaning God's provision for your life.

As a woman of wisdom, you understand that life is ebb and flow. Therefore, being content over time should become more manageable. Woman of Wisdom, whatever the season, follow Paul's example. Learn to appreciate the season you're in, rather young or old, plenty or in need, lonely or alone, happy or sad. Each season is a blessing.

The Bible states in Philippians 4:11 *"I am not saying this because I am in need, for I have learned to be content whatever the circumstances."*

It's your life, so live it! Love and hugs, MiMi.

Song of the day - Seasons Change - by United Pursuit.

Thoughts

Inspiration for Today

Beautiful Woman of Wisdom,

Life has seasons; there are times you'll have plenty, times you lack, times of joy and tears. It's called LIFE. When living through a season of uncertainty, you can take comfort in the Lord as you wait for your season to change. Everything must change!

Isaiah 40:31 *"Yet those who wait for The Lord will gain new strength; they will mount up with wings like eagles, they will run and not get tired, they will walk and not become weary." It's your life, so live it with hope and faith. Be assured that the sun will shine again.*

It's your life, so live it! Love and hugs, MiMi.

Song of the day - Sun will shine again - by Michelle Williams

Thoughts

Inspiration for Today

Beautiful Woman of Wisdom,

Do you have the illusion that you deserve a problem-free life? If so, that is wrong thinking. As a woman, you can expect to experience a mixture of good and bad, ups and downs, and rounds and rounds. Some of your life situations happen because of your choices; you became weary, couldn't see your way clear, trusted the wrong person, or just plain confused.

No matter the state you find yourself in, remember it's your life, so live it. Fight to live another day, fight through the situation, and keep in mind that no weapon form against you will prosper. It may form, but it won't prosper.

Mo Isiah 54:17 *"No weapon formed against you will prevail, and you will refute every tongue that accuses you. This is the heritage of the servants of the LORD, and this is their vindication from me," declares the LORD."*

1 Peter 5:6-7 *"Humble yourselves, therefore, under the mighty hand of God so that at the proper time, he may exalt you, casting all your anxieties on him, because he cares for you."*

It's your life, so live it! Love and hugs, MiMi.

Song of the day - No weapon formed against me will prosper - by Fred Hammond

Thoughts

Inspiration for Today

Beautiful Woman of Wisdom,

You will experience trials and tribulations in your lifetime; but, you know that trouble doesn't last always, and if you hold on to God's hand, you will make it through.

When you go through your trials, he will be there with you to protect, strengthen and provide you with peace and love.

James 1:2-5 *"My brethren, count it all joy when you fall into various trials, knowing that the testing of your faith produces patience. But let patience have its perfect work, that you may be perfect and complete, lacking nothing."*

It's your life, so live it! Love and hugs, MiMi.

Song of the day - God Favored Me - by Hezekiah Walker

Thought

Inspiration for Today

Beautiful Woman of Wisdom,

It's your life, and you need to live it on purpose. Have you become fearful and anxious in this season of life? When you enter an uncertain season, it can cause stress, and you may become anxious.

Your approach is essential; you can walk through it exercising your faith or mess it up by trying to fix it yourself. Wisdom tells you to walk it out, but stress tells you to try and fix it.

I believe you subject yourself to unnecessary stress and pressure when you try and enforce your will into a situation. Take your hand off the wheel and let God lead you. Today, I challenge you to let go and let God.

Ephesians 3:20 *"Now to Him who is able to do far more abundantly beyond all that we ask or think, according to the power that works within us,"*

It's your life, so live it! Love and hugs, MiMi.

Song of the day - Let go and let God - by Keith Wonder boy Johnson

Thoughts

Inspiration for Today

Beautiful Woman of Wisdom,

The importance of using wisdom in your daily life is crucial to a prosperous and peaceful life! Although it seems challenging for you to exercise godly attributes of knowledge, governing your words, slow to anger, showing humility, a forgiving spirit, a calm spirit, it's not too late, so why not try?

How are you living? Remember, it's your life, so live it wisely. Apply life lessons to your daily walk and use the knowledge you've obtained over the years.

Proverbs 10:28 *"The prospect of the righteous is joy, but the hopes of the wicked come to nothing!*

It's your life, so live it! Love and hugs, MiMi.

Song of the day - Perfect - by Marvin Sapp

Thoughts

Inspiration for Today

Beautiful Woman of Wisdom

Proverbs 31:29-30 *"Many woman have done excellently, but you surpass them all. Charm is deceitful, and beauty is vain, but a woman who fears the Lord is to be praised."*

It's your life, so live it. Live a faithful and meaningful life that is pleasing to our Heavenly Father. You have the gift of life; you have the blessing of a new day, so live on purpose. What is your vision for your life?

Prayer

Father, help us to walk before you in fear and admonition. Teach us to lose ourselves in you. So that our praise is pure and our service is yours. Amen.

Don't stop moving towards the vision. Love and hugs, MiMi.

Song of the day -Virtuous Woman - by Flavour

Thoughts

PART THREE:

30 DAYS OF YOUR VISION

Inspiration for Today

Beautiful Woman of Wisdom,

For the last 60 days, you've read that each day is new and that it's your life, so live it. What's next? Where are you going? What's your vision for your life?

Vision defined by Webster "is the ability to see something that you imagine a picture you see in your mind, something that you've dreamed, especially as part of a religious or supernatural experience."

A vision is a plan, a goal, a dream; it's an assignment from God. There is so much more to your vision than the definition. It involves walking by faith, having unwavering hope, and the tenacity to go after it! What's your vision?

Mark 11 :24 *"Therefore I tell you, whatever you ask for in prayer, believe that you have received it, and it will be yours."*

Don't stop moving towards the vision. Love and hugs, MiMi.

Song of the day - The Vision - by Patrick Love

Thoughts

Inspiration for Today

Beautiful Woman of Wisdom,

Reading the story of Eve recaptures the difficulty of listening to the voice of God and following His direction. Often, you go your own way and find yourself on the wrong path. It's hard at times to hear the voice of God to drown out the noise in your lives; influences from everywhere interferes with your listening.

Take heart the Lord cares, and He is right there listening.

Deuteronomy 31:8 speaks to that fact, ***"It is the Lord who goes before you. He will be with you; he will not leave you or forsake you. Do not fear or be dismayed."***

You may now continue on your path, walking towards your vision with less noise.

Don't stop moving toward the vision. Love and hugs, MiMi.

Song of the day – Lord do it - by Hezekiah Walker.

Thoughts

Inspiration for Today

Beautiful Woman of Wisdom,

Vision distractors, what's yours? Do you overthink the process, procrastinate, and waste time on nothingness? How do you deal with the distractions of life? Are there things that you don't realize are distracting you from working your vision?

It's wise to regularly take an inventory of your lives, reflecting inwardly and taking stock of your plan. The most important attribute needed to see the vision through is your faith. You serve a mighty God who journeys with you and always has your best in mind.

Mark 4:19 *"But all too quickly the message is crowded out by the worries of this life, the lure of wealth, and the desire for other things, so no fruit is produced."*

Don't stop moving toward the vision. Love and hugs, MiMi.

Song of the day - Be Thou My Vision - by Selah.

Thoughts

Inspiration for Today

Beautiful Woman of Wisdom,

Determination is key to reaching your destination; make up your mind and work diligently daily. The truth is, regardless of what's written or what words of encouragement you hear, if you're not committed to the Lord, the goal, the vision, nothing will manifest.

Many years have gone by, and you are still speaking of your weight loss goal, educational goal, family dream, or writing a book. The time is now!

You can be your worst distraction; you need to take a step back and assess how often you allow distractions into your time. Be a bit selfish, bold, and determine to make this day successful. Make time for the Lord and work towards the manifestation of your vision.

Proverbs 16:3 *"Commit to the LORD whatever you do, and he will establish your plans."*

Psalm 37:5 *"Commit your way to the LORD; trust in him, and he will do this."*

Don't stop moving toward the vision. Love and hugs, MiMi.

Song of the day - Still I Rise - by Yolanda Adams.

Thoughts

Inspiration for Today

Beautiful Woman of Wisdom,

How exciting it is to have a vision from God?

Isaiah 6:8 *"Then I heard the voice of the Lord saying, "Whom shall I send? And who will go for us?" And I said, "Here am I. Send me!"*

The beauty of a God-given vision! When you allow the world to consume you, you begin to stray away from the vision, the plan that God has for you. The dream starts to become secondary to the things of the world, and your vision loses its worth. Whatever it takes to continue to work towards the plan is what you need to do. Focus on the task, put in the work, and stay the course. The Lord is with you every step of the way.

"Vision without action is merely a dream. Action without vision just passes the time. Vision with action can change the world." Joel A. Barker

Don't stop moving toward the vision. Love and hugs, MiMi.

Song of the day – You know my name – by Tasha Cobbs.

Thoughts

Inspiration for Today

Beautiful Woman of Wisdom,

Are you feeling energized today? Do you feel like you can take on the world? The world meaning that endless to-do list. Does your to-do-list include working on your vision or the things of God? It's understandable to want to do it all, but is it feasible? It becomes overwhelming, and most times, accomplishing **it all** becomes impossible.

Steady as she goes is the instruction from the captain to the helmsman of a ship to keep the ship heading steadily on the same course regardless of gusts of wind or cross-current. That is how you must navigate your lives steady and consistent against all obstacles. Where do you start? Reorganize your to-do list remove things, step back and reflect.

Isaiah 41:10 *"Fear not, for I am with you; be not dismayed, for I am your God; I will strengthen you, I will help you, I will uphold you with my righteous right hand."*

Don't stop moving toward the vision. Love and hugs, MiMi.

Song of the day - New Day – Danny Gokey

Thoughts

Inspiration for Today

Beautiful Woman of Wisdom,

Are you there yet? Remember the movie that Ice Cube starred in; the film is about a journey and the things that happen along the way. In the same vein, I'm asking, "Are you there yet?" Where is there? It's the manifestation of your vision.

Is your journey bumpy, smooth, fun, sad, or challenging? Don't be discouraged. That's Life! The beauty of a journey is what you experience along the way. Enjoy!

John 10:10 *"The thief comes only to steal and kill and destroy. I came that they may have life and have it abundantly."*

Don't stop moving toward the vision. Love and hugs, MiMi.

Song of the day - Encourage Yourself - by Donald Lawrence

Thoughts

Inspiration for Today

Beautiful Woman of Wisdom,

The Lord is the author and finisher of your faith. However, you have free will, freedom to decide which path you take. It isn't important how you started or where you are at this moment in life.

It's a new day, and the Lord has given a second, third, and fourth chance to start again. My Sisters continue walking towards your vision.

The Word of God says,

Hebrews 12:2 *"Keep your eyes on Jesus, whom both began and finished this race."*

2 Chronicles 15:7 *"But as for you, be strong and do not give up, for your work will be rewarded."*

Psalm 20:4 *"May he give you the desire of your heart and make all your plans succeed."*

Don't stop moving toward the vision. Love and hugs, MiMi.

Song of the day - Never Gave Up - by Tasha Cobbs Leonard

Thoughts

Inspiration for Today

Beautiful Woman of Wisdom,

Have you ever felt like you weren't good enough for your vision although you have the passion? Have you been around a group of people and thought to yourself, I shouldn't be here? Why am I here, Lord?

It's normal to have some reservations when moving into your vision but do not stop pushing forward. Kingdom building requires each of us to walk in faith and proceed with passion and purpose into our future.

Timothy 1:7 "For God hath not given us the spirit of fear; but of power, and of love, and of a sound mind."

Don't stop moving toward the vision. Love and hugs, MiMi.

Song of the day - Breathe - by Byron Cage

Thoughts

Inspiration for Today

Beautiful Woman of Wisdom,

Conditioning, there are many ways to condition yourselves. You can condition your hair, bodies, and mind. Your thoughts, actions, and beliefs come from a lifetime of conditioning from many sources but mainly from childhood influences.

Conditioned beliefs are the thinking patterns developed at a young age; usually, they're in place by the start of school. They become the foundation for your future decision-making and problem-solving. If you find that your conditioning is contrary to the life you desire through faith, prayer, and hard work, it can change. All things are possible!

Proverbs 16:3 *"Commit to the LORD whatever you do, and he will establish your plans."*

Don't stop moving toward the vision. Love and hugs, MiMi.

Song of the day - Great is Your Mercy - by Donnie McClurkin.

Thoughts

Inspiration for Today

Beautiful Woman of Wisdom,

Today is dedicated to you, beautiful Sister; you continue to shine bright although your path has given you darkness. You continue to press your way forward despite the effort it takes to push. You continue to love others despite the pain they may have caused you. You continue to hope despite what you see and hear. You continue towards your vision, and you continue to shine! You are beautiful!

1 Peter 3:3-4 *"Your beauty should not come from outward adornments, such as elaborate hairstyles and the wearing of gold jewelry or fine clothes. Rather, it should be that of your inner self, the unfading beauty of a gentle and quiet spirit, which is of great worth in God's sight."*

Don't stop moving toward the vision. Love and hugs, MiMi.

Song of the day – Beautiful - by Mali Music

Thoughts

Inspiration for Today

Beautiful Woman of Wisdom,

The Lord knows our name; He knows every part of us from head to toe in every internal part of us. He has a vision for our life; your vision may not look like the next woman, but it's a call to your vision, and together God's will for humanity will come to fruition through the many purposes.

Some of us may look at another woman and say, wow, she got it all worked out; what about me, Lord? We only see the result, not the whole story; we can learn from each other, share our story, and encourage the next woman.

Psalm 139:13-16 *"For you formed my inward parts; you knitted me together in my mother's womb. I praise you, for I am fearfully and wonderfully made. Wonderful are your works; my soul knows it very well. My frame was not hidden from you when I was being made in secret, intricately woven in the depths of the earth. Your eyes saw my unformed substance; in your book were written, every one of them, the days that were formed for me, when as yet there was none of them. "*

Don't stop moving toward the vision. Love and hugs, MiMi.

Song of the day - Struggle Gospel Reggae 2020 - by Cudjoe

Thoughts

Inspiration for Today

Beautiful Woman of Wisdom,

No matter what word you choose to use, growth or change, it equals progress. You are writing the story of your life, and when you look at your life, do you see growth? What does your story say about how you lived?

Does it seem that you're reading the same chapter over and over again? Procrastination? Loss of faith? Un-forgiveness? Search your story and write your ending. Write the vision and make it a plan.

1 Peter 3:10-11 (MSG) *"Whoever wants to embrace life and see the day fill up with good, here's what you do: Say nothing evil or hurtful; Snub evil and cultivate good; run after peace for all you're worth."*

Don't stop moving toward the vision. Love and hugs, MiMi.

Song of the day - The Prayer - by Donnie McClurkin & Yolanda Adams

Thoughts

Inspiration for Today

Beautiful Woman of Wisdom,

Do it now! Be intentional about your growth, dreams, and aspirations. If you say tomorrow, I will do this or that tomorrow may never come. Do it now! Go after your vision.

Often you say I need motivation, or I am not motivated; if you start, you're farther than you were, and inspiration will follow. Do you believe it? Remember that time is short, and it is later in the evening than you may realize.

Proverbs 6:4-11 *"Don't put it off. Do it now! Don't rest until you do. Save yourself like a deer escaping from a hunter, like a bird fleeing from a net. Take a lesson from the ants, you lazybones. Learn from their ways and be wise! Even though they have no prince, governor, or ruler to make them work, they labor hard all summer, gathering food for the winter. But you, lazybones, how long will you sleep? When will you wake up? I want you to learn this lesson: A little extra sleep, a little more slumber, a little folding of the hands to rest -- and poverty will pounce on you like a bandit; scarcity will attack you like an armed robber."*

Don't stop moving toward the vision. Love and hugs, MiMi.

Song of the day - Break Every Chain - by Tasha Cobbs

Thoughts

Inspiration for Today

Beautiful Woman of Wisdom,

Preparation! When preparing for a date, you set the atmosphere, ensuring you look just right; when preparing for the club or church, you make sure you're on point after all people are looking.

You put so much thought into those things. What about your life? How do you set the atmosphere? How do you prepare for your day, the week, your journey? Setting the atmosphere for life is crucial to success and the manifestation of the vision.

The 23rd Psalm will certainly prepare us for our journey. *"The Lord is my Shepherd: I shall not want that will certainly set the atmosphere because you lack nothing it allows us to cruise through your day even if your pockets are empty, and your refrigerators are bare. He leads me beside quiet waters; He refreshes my soul. He guides me along the right paths for his name's sake. This will give us peace throughout your day; knowing the Lord refreshes and leads will give us peace. Even though I walk through the darkest valley, I will fear no evil, for you are with me; your rod and your staff, they comfort me. Even if you are in a tight place, the Lord is your rod and staff. You prepare a table before me in the presence of my enemies. You anoint my head with oil; my cup overflows. The preparation is completed you overflow. Surely your goodness and love will follow me all the days of my life, and I will dwell in the house of the Lord forever."*

The atmosphere *is set; you* may now proceed with your life.

Don't stop moving toward the vision. Love and hugs, MiMi.

Song of the day - 23rd Psalm - by Jeff Majors

Thoughts

Inspiration for Today

Beautiful Woman with Wisdom,

Your Voice! Are you using your voice for your passion? Passion is a strong feeling of enthusiasm or excitement for something or about doing something.

What is your passion? Do you have a passion for something or anything? If so, what are you doing about it?

The power behind all great art, all great music, all great books, the driving force behind a great movie, and all great paintings is *passion*. Fuel your vision with passion. Do you realize that your vision could make a difference in others' lives, and your voice could become the link between you and the world? Make an impact!

Mark 12:30-31 *"and you must love the Lord your God with all your heart, all your soul, all your mind, and all your strength.' The second is equally important: 'Love your neighbor as yourself."*

Don't stop moving toward the vision. Love and hugs, MiMi.

Song of the day - Go Make a Difference - by Steve Angrisano & Tom Tomaszek.

Thoughts

Inspiration for Today

Beautiful Woman with Wisdom,

Is today going to be successful? How will you make today successful when life keeps happening? By His Grace!

God's grace will help you move through the day; His love will give you the strength to succeed.

"You cannot earn what God gives us; you cannot deserve it; what God gives us is given out of the goodness of his heart; what God gives is not pay, but a gift; not a reward, but a grace." William Barclay

Psalm 45:2 ***"You are the most excellent of men, and your lips have been anointed with grace since God has blessed you forever."***

Ephesians 4:7 ***"But to each one of us grace has been given as Christ apportioned it."***

Don't stop moving toward the vision. Love and hugs, MiMi.

Song of the day – Yes I will – by Vertical Worship

Thoughts

234

Inspiration for Today

Beautiful Woman of Wisdom,

The objective is to see your vision manifest. It will take wisdom to see the plan through. It's vital to use discernment when making decisions in your life. How do you accomplish this? Ask for wisdom.

James 1:5 *"If any of you lacks wisdom, he should ask God, who gives generously to all without finding fault, and it will be given to him."*

Proverbs 31:26 *"She opens her mouth with wisdom, and the teaching of kindness is on her tongue."*

Proverbs 8: 1-3 *"Can't you hear the voice of wisdom? She is standing at the city gates and at every fork in the road, and at the door of every house. Listen to what she says:"*

Don't stop moving toward the vision. Love and hugs, MiMi.

Song of the day - You're a Daughter of God - by Walk Tall

Thoughts

Inspiration for Today

Beautiful Woman with Wisdom,

It's easy to fall by the wayside, depending on what you're dealing with in life. Falling by the wayside means you fail to persist in an endeavor or undertaking, goals, or commitments. There will be times when falling by the wayside will pull you back to old behaviors.

When this happens, prayer and faith are your weapons of defense. Know that your fall is not permanent and that Lord is faithful and ever-present.

Proverb 3:5 *"Trust in the Lord with all of your heart, and lean not on your own understanding."*

Don't stop moving toward the vision. Love and hugs, MiMi.

Song of the day - Don't give up - by Kirk Franklin, Hezekiah Walker, Donald Lawrence and Karen Clark

Thoughts

Inspiration for Today

Beautiful Woman of Wisdom,

Focused and Fearless Woman of Wisdom, you are daughters of the Most-High, strong and capable of completing the assignment. You may be thinking, how can I be fearless? It's normal to have fears. The answer to that question is yes, it's normal to have fears. However, it's not expected as a Daughter of the Most-High to walk an unfocused and fearful life. Living this way is contrary to the gift of love, faith, and the promise of God.

Being focused means "directing a great deal of attention, interest, or activity towards a particular aim." If you focus on your goals, dreams, and vision, there will be little time for fear. When you understand where you are and where you are going, your fear will subside. The Bible offers powerful scriptures for those unpleasant thoughts and voices that hinder us from a Focused and Fearless life. "Do not be afraid."

Daniel 4:5 *"I saw a dream, and it made me fearful, and these fantasies as I lay on my bed and the visions in my mind kept alarming me.*

Don't stop moving toward the vision. Love and hugs, MiMi.

Song of the day - I Call You Faithful - Donnie McClurkin lyrics

Thoughts

Inspiration for Today

Beautiful Woman of Wisdom,

Many women have come before us, and because they lived, our road is less bumpy, and new doors have opened. The path we take can make the lives of those behind us more comfortable. Look deeply at your life and the legacy you're building. It's not important how big the vision is; what matters is the purpose and impact.

Just think, what if Rehab had not hidden the spies in Joshua 2:3? What if Susan B. Anthony, American Campaigner against slavery and for the promotion of woman's and worker's rights decided to take a different path? What if Maya Angelou, poet and award-winning author, decided not to write, inspire and share her gifts with the world?

Perhaps our path is not as grand as these women, but our course is important and makes a difference.

Proverb 4:11 ***"I instruct you in the way of wisdom and lead you along straight paths."***

Don't stop moving toward the vision. Love and hugs, MiMi.

Song of the day – Legacy - by Nichole Nordeman

Thoughts

Inspiration for Today

Beautiful Woman of Wisdom,

Legacy, what legacy will you leave behind?

I read an article by Bill High, where he stated, *"Faithfulness is the heart of legacy. It is the idea that you'll be faithful with what you've been given. God has entrusted financial resources, but He has also entrusted you with far more valuable things: your families and your ability to influence them (and others) for good."*

What's most important how you live or how you lived? How you live determines the legacy, you leave behind, and how you have lived is your legacy. When you talk about how you live, are you living recklessly, believing you have another day to do better?

I'll do it tomorrow; there may be no tomorrow. Building a legacy is a work in progress, which means working on it.

Benjamin Franklin once said, ***"If you would not be forgotten as soon as you are dead, either write something worth reading or do something worth writing."***

Philippians 4:13 *"I can do all things through him who strengthens me."*

Don't stop moving toward the vision. Love and hugs, MiMi.

Song of the day - Tomorrow - by The Winans and Tamia Perform

Thoughts

Inspiration for Today

Beautiful Woman of Wisdom,

The Word of God declares that you are beautiful.

"You are altogether beautiful, my darling; there is no flaw in you. Charm is deceptive, and beauty is fleeting, but a woman who fears the Lord is to be praised."

There will be days when you are at your worst; you doubt yourselves, and you doubt God. You question yourselves, "am I good enough? Some days, it's hard to see the inward beauty you see a flawed woman, a failing woman; this is when you must remember how God sees you.

You are beautifully flawed.

Proverbs 31:25 *"She is clothed with strength and dignity; she can laugh at the days to come."*

Proverbs 31:26 *"She opens her mouth with wisdom, and the teaching of kindness is on her tongue."*

Isaiah 62:3 *"You will be a crown of splendor in the LORD's hand, a royal diadem in the hand of your God."*

Don't stop moving toward the vision. Love and hugs, MiMi.

Song of the day - Alabaster Box- by CeCe Winans

Thoughts

Inspiration for Today

Beautiful Woman of Wisdom,

You are on a journey, and your destination is the manifestation of your vision. Hopefully, with each step you take, you're closer to your goal.

To accomplish your vision, it will take showing yourself generosity.

This means taking the time to care for yourselves and working on your goals. Others may see your generosity towards yourselves as selfishness or neglecting time with them. It's important to be okay with taking time for yourself, your dreams, and the things of God.

1 John 2:15 *"Love not the world, neither the things that are in the world. If any man love the world, the love of the Father is not in him."*

Don't stop moving toward the vision. Love and hugs, MiMi.

Song for the day – Jehovah you are Most High God – by Dr. Kofi Thompson

Thoughts

Inspiration for Today

Beautiful Woman of Wisdom,

Foolishness is when you act without using wisdom or common sense when you make foolish decisions or repeat the same mistakes. An act of foolishness is sometimes called folly in the Bible.

Proverbs 26:4-5 *"Answer not a fool according to his folly, lest you be like him yourself. Answer a fool according to his folly, lest he is wise in his own eyes."*

How often has The Lord's faithfulness saved you in your time of foolishness? How many times have you made the same decisions and expected a different result? That's insanity, meaning doing the same thing over and over again and expecting different results." This foolish cycle will interfere with the manifestation of the vision and life.

2 Samuel 24:10 *"Now David's heart troubled him after he had numbered the people, So David said to the LORD, "I have sinned greatly in what I have done But now, O LORD, please take away the iniquity of Your servant, for I have acted very foolishly."*

Don't stop moving toward the vision. Love and hugs, MiMi.

Song of the day - Great is your Mercy - by Donnie McClurkin

Thoughts

Inspiration for Today

Beautiful Woman of Wisdom,

Inconsistent is the act of being erratic, changeable, or unpredictable. Have you thought about your life, your walk, your ways? Your walk with the Lord should always be consistent; you can't allow day-to-day life issues to influence your walk.

The longer you walk closely with God, the better you will know him. He will continually open your eyes to His will and enable the manifestation of the vision.

Romans 13:13 *"Let us walk with decency, as in the daylight: not in carousing and drunkenness; not in sexual impurity and promiscuity; not in quarreling and jealousy."*

Ephesians 2:*10 "For you are His creation, created in Christ Jesus for good works, which God prepared ahead of time so that you should walk in them."*

Don't stop moving toward the vision. Love and hugs, MiMi.

Song of the day - Just a Closer Walk with Thee - by Mahalia Jackson

Thoughts

Inspiration for Today

Beautiful Woman of Wisdom,

INCONSISTENT!

I will venture to say that each of us has experienced an inconsistent walk with the Lord in our lifetime. Time is lost when our walk with the Lord becomes inconsistent.

What does it mean to walk consistently with The Lord? It means you trust Him in all circumstances, even in those times of plenty, lack, sickness, loss, confusion, and depression.

Philippians 4:11-13 *"Not that I speak from want, for I have learned to be content in whatever circumstances I am."*

Don't stop moving toward the vision. Love and hugs, MiMi.

Song of the day - This is my Exodus - by Donald Lawrence.

Thoughts

Inspiration for Today

Beautiful Woman of Wisdom,

No time is ever enough! The importance of how you use your time grows more important with age. You believe you have all the time in the world, I want to caution you; Matthew 24:36 states ***"But about that day or hour no one knows, not even the angels in heaven, nor the Son, but only the Father."***

Let's not waste time on foolishness, dead-ends, or people who add no value to our lives. Wasted time interferes with the manifestation of the vision and the plan the Lord has given; don't waste a moment of your precious time.

"Life unfolds in the present." But so often, you let the present slip away, allowing time to rush past unobserved and unseized, and squandering the precious seconds of your lives as you worry about the future and ruminate about what's past."

The Art of Now

Don't stop moving toward the vision. Love and hugs, MiMi.

Song of the day - Don't waste your time - by Tia Campbell.

Thoughts

Inspiration for Today

Beautiful Woman of Wisdom,

The vision is assigned; nothing is stopping us except ourselves. Horatio Spafford is the writer of the beloved song "It is well with my Soul" He tells the story of a significant loss financially and personally, yet he was able to say "It is well" regardless of what you're facing in life, you must complete the assignment.

Of course, you won't be able to say everything is well in your lives, always. You will face challenges and perhaps tragedies, but with faith and hope in the promises of God, you will say it is well.

Romans 15:13 **"May the God of hope fill you with all joy and peace as you trust in him, so that you may overflow with hope by the power of the Holy Spirit."**

Don't stop moving toward the vision. Love and hugs, MiMi.

Song of the day – Another Day's Journey – by Lashun Pace

Thoughts

Inspiration for Today

Beautiful Woman of Wisdom,

I pray that you have gained a deeper understanding of the simplicity of connecting with God. There is a quote, *"Scripture is like a river . . . broad and deep, shallow enough for the lamb to go wading, but deep enough for the elephant to swim."* Grateful to the Dead

It's just that simple don't overcomplicate it. The scriptures will meet you where you are. Keep in mind that becoming a woman of wisdom is a work in progress; as I define it, the definition is growing daily using your God-given wisdom in every situation of your life.

"Proverbs 3:13 *"happy is the woman who finds wisdom and the woman who gets understanding."*

Enjoy each new day, celebrate life, and don't stop until the vision comes to fruition.

I genuinely love each of you and want nothing but God's best for your life.

MiMi.